Hey Jack! Books

First American Edition 2014
Kane Miller, A Division of EDC Publishing

Text copyright © 2013 Sally Rippin
Illustration copyright © 2013 Stephanie Spartels
Logo and design copyright © 2013 Hardie Grant Egmont

For information contact:
Kane Miller, A Division of EDC Publishing
P.O. Box 470663
Tulsa, OK 74147-0663
www.kanemiller.com
www.edcpub.com
www.usbornebooksandmore.com

Library of Congress Control Number: 2013944867

Printed and bound in the United States of America
4 5 6 7 8 9 10
ISBN: 978-1-61067-259-7

Hey Jack!

The Top Team

By Sally Rippin

Illustrated by Stephanie Spartels

Kane Miller
A DIVISION OF EDC PUBLISHING

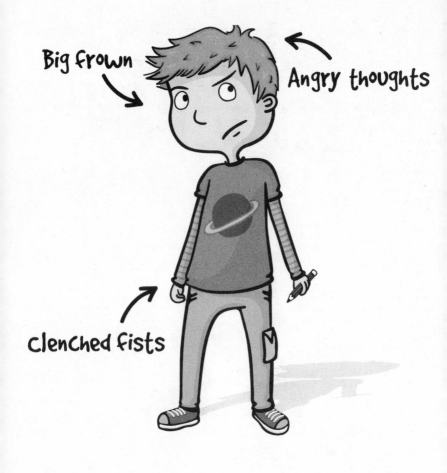

Big frown

Angry thoughts

clenched fists

Grouchy Mood

Chapter One

This is Jack.

Today Jack is in a grouchy mood.

Ms. Walton has put him on a team with Alex.

Usually Jack works with Billie.

"Do I have to work with Alex?" Jack asks Ms. Walton. "Can't I work with Billie?"

"Not today, Jack," says Ms. Walton. "I think you and Alex will make a good team."

Jack sighs and gives
Billie a sad little wave.
She waves back.

This week is Math Week. Jack's class is having a competition.

The winning team gets a set of glow-in-the-dark stickers. Jack loves glow-in-the-dark stickers. He **really** wants to win.

Jack and Alex start their first math task. It is an adding and subtracting game.

Jack and Alex work out the answers in their heads. But Alex is always faster. He writes the answers down before Jack can even start.

"Hey, let me do some,"

Jack says crossly.

"All right. You do the next one then," says Alex.

Jack looks at the math problem. It is a very **tricky** one. He is not sure if he should take away or add.

He starts writing down an answer.

7

"That's not right,"
Alex says. He takes the
pencil away from Jack.

"Hey, I'm not finished!"
shouts Jack. He **grabs**
the pencil.

"But you can't do it!"
Alex yells.

"Boys!" says Ms. Walton.

8

She walks over.

"What's going on?"

"Alex won't let me answer any questions," Jack complains.

"He's getting them wrong!" Alex says.

"You boys have to work together or you will lose points," Ms. Walton says.

She walks to the front of the class.

Jack frowns at Alex. He **hates** getting in trouble. Especially when it's not his fault! Why does he have to be on a team with Alex? He and Billie make a much better team.

Alex frowns at Jack and
hands him the pencil.
"Look, it's like this
question up here," he says.

He still sounds a
bit grumpy.

Jack does the problem
again and writes
down his answer.
Alex nods and gives
a little smile.

At the end of the lesson,
Ms. Walton reads out
the answers.

Jack and Alex only got two wrong.

One of them was Jack's answer and one was Alex's.

Jack and Alex are **winning**. Billie and Mika are coming second.

Jack grins happily.

So does Alex.

They give each other
a **high five**.

Maybe being on a team with Alex isn't so bad after all, Jack thinks.

Chapter Two

The next day in math,
Jack sits next to Alex
again. Today is division.
Jack frowns.
Division is hard.

He can never remember where to put the numbers.

Jack watches Alex do the first problem. Then Alex hands him the pencil.

"I'm not very good at division," says Jack shyly. "Maybe you should do these ones?"

Alex shakes his head.
"Remember what
Ms. Walton said?

We have to do them together or we'll lose points. Look, just watch me. It's easy," he says **kindly**.

Jack watches Alex do the next problem. *Hmmm,* he thinks. *That doesn't look too hard.*

"All right," he says. "I'll have a try." He copies what Alex did.

"Yes!" says Alex. "You've got it!"

Jack grins. He hands the pencil back to Alex.

The two boys take turns to do the whole page of problems.

If Jack gets **Stuck**, Alex shows him where the numbers go. They are finished in no time.

Ms. Walton reads out
the answers.

Today they only get
two wrong answers.
Billie and Mika's
team only get two
wrong too.

But Jack and Alex are
still in the lead!

All week, the boys work
together on their math
problems.

Sometimes Alex has to show Jack how to do a problem. But usually Jack can work out the answers by himself.

By the end of the week, their team is ahead by ten points! Jack feels very **proud**.

"Woo hoo!" Jack says.
He runs up to Billie after
class. "We're win-ning!
We're win-ning!" he says
in a sing-song voice.

Billie frowns. "You're only winning because you have Alex on your team," she says. "Everyone knows that Alex is the best at math."

Jack **gasps**. "That's not true! Alex just shows me how to do the first one. Then I copy him.

I'm still doing the problems by myself."

Billie crosses her arms and glares at Jack. "Well you must be copying him by being a show-off, too!" she huffs, then walks away.

Jack feels **upset** that Billie is so cross at him. Then he frowns.

She's just jealous because

we're winning! he thinks.

Chapter Three

Today is the last
day of Math Week.
Ms. Walton hands
out the math sheets.
Oh no! thinks Jack.

Multiplication! That's my worst.

Jack watches Alex do the first problem. Then Alex hands him the pencil.

"I can't do these," Jack whispers. "You do them."

Alex shakes his head. "Ms. Walton said we have to work together, remember?"

32

Jack's face turns red.

He pushes the paper

towards Alex. "No!

We'll lose if I do them.

Quick, you do them,

Alex. We're running out

of time!"

But Alex just pushes the

paper back to Jack.

Jack frowns. He looks at the problems, but he can't work them out. They are too hard. He is terrible at multiplication.

He quickly writes down half of the answers as best as he can. Alex does the other half.

"OK, class," says Ms. Walton. "Time's up!" She reads out the answers.

Alex only gets two answers wrong. But Jack only gets two right.

35

He hangs his head. Jack and Alex have lost the competition.

"Sorry, Alex," Jack says. "It's my fault. You would have won without me."

"It doesn't matter!" Alex says. "Winning isn't everything! I had fun working with you, Jack."

"Really?" says Jack.

"Yeah, really!" says Alex. He smiles and Jack feels **warm** inside.

"We won! We won!"
Billie and Mika sing
happily. Billie makes a
funny face at Jack.

Jack laughs.

Billie laughs too.

"Hold on," Ms. Walton says. "Not so fast. This week was also about teamwork. Jack and Alex, you remember how I told you I would take points off if you didn't work together?"

Jack and Alex nod.

"Well, I think you two have worked very well as a team. So I would like to award you an **extra** ten points."

Jack looks down at the paper. This is an easy problem. He quickly adds ten points to their score. Jack and Alex's team now has the same number of points as Billie and Mika's team. It's a tie!

Jack and Alex jump up and down with excitement.

Ms. Walton smiles.

She gives one package
of stickers to Billie's
team. And one package
of stickers to Jack's team.

After school, Billie and Jack walk home together.

Billie **grins** and puts her arm around Jack. "I'm glad it was a tie," she says.

"Me too," says Jack. "But I'm even more glad that we are friends again."